Flubby Does Not Like Snow

To my editor, Renee Kelly, and the great team
at Penguin Workshop for all that they do—JEM

PENGUIN WORKSHOP
An imprint of Penguin Random House LLC, New York

First published simultaneously in paperback and hardcover in the United States of America by
Penguin Workshop, an imprint of Penguin Random House LLC, New York, 2023

Visit us online at penguinrandomhouse.com.

Library of Congress Cataloging-in-Publication Data is available.

Manufactured in China

ISBN 9780593523384 (pbk)

10 9 8 7 6 5 4 3 2 1 TOPL

Flubby Does Not Like Snow

Like Snow

by J. E. Morris

Penguin Workshop

"Look, Flubby. It is snowing!"

It snowed a little.

Then it snowed a lot!

I have an idea.

Let's go outside.

We can play in the snow.

Playing in the snow is fun!

11

Flubby goes outside.

The snow is cold.

Flubby's feet are cold.

Flubby does not like snow.

So he goes back inside.

Here are some boots.

Boots will keep Flubby's
feet warm.

Now Flubby will play
in the snow.

Flubby goes outside.

But his back is cold.

So he goes back inside.

Here is a coat.

A coat will keep Flubby's
back warm.

Now Flubby will play
in the snow.

Flubby goes outside.

But his head is cold.

So he goes back inside.

Here is a hat and scarf.

A hat and scarf will keep
Flubby's head warm.

Now Flubby will play
in the snow.

Flubby goes outside.

His feet are warm.

His back is warm.

And Flubby's head
is warm.

So he does NOT go
back inside.

Flubby likes playing
in the snow.

Playing in the snow is fun!